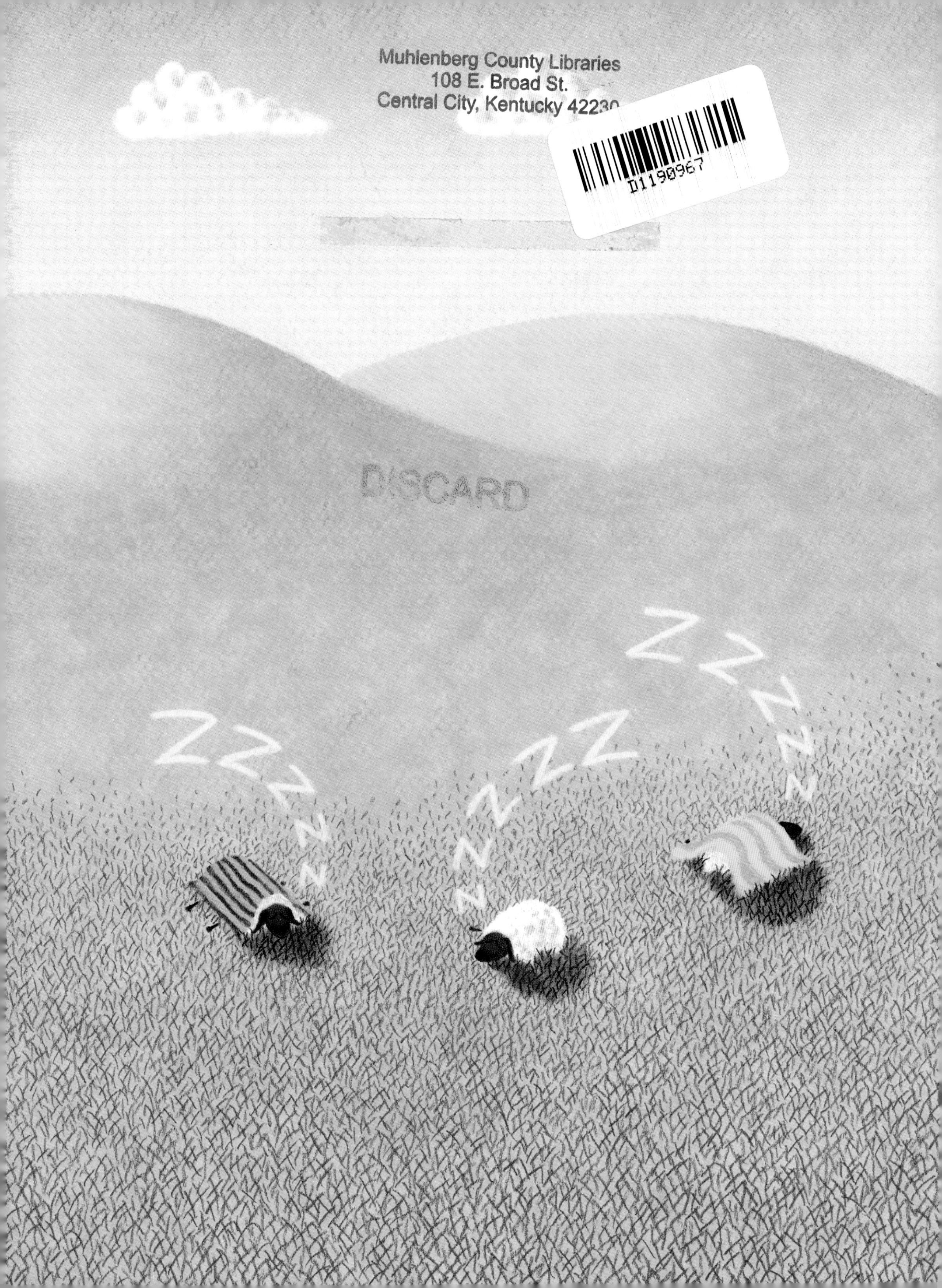

SIMPSON'S SHEEP JUST WANT TO SLEEP!

Bruce Arant

 PETER PAUPER PRESS, INC.
White Plains, New York

To my family flock . . . My wife Dawn, for her patience and support, and to my kids Arliss, Kate, and Collin

Thanks once again for the guidance and expertise of my agent Marie Galastro of MLG & Associates LLC.

Designed by Heather Zschock

Published by Peter Pauper Press, Inc.
202 Mamaroneck Avenue
White Plains, New York 10601 USA

Published in the United Kingdom and Europe by Peter Pauper Press, Inc.
c/o White Pebble International
Unit 2, Plot 11 Terminus Rd.
Chichester, West Sussex PO19 8TX, UK

Library of Congress Cataloging-in-Publication Data Available

ISBN 978-1-4413-2429-0
Manufactured for Peter Pauper Press, Inc.
Printed in Hong Kong

7 6 5 4 3 2 1

Visit us at www.peterpauper.com

SIMPSON'S SHEEP
JUST WANT TO SLEEP!

Farmer Simpson sleeps all night
in comfy blankets, cuddled tight.
He lies in bed and softly snores,
while dreaming dreams of doing chores.

At last the sun turns night to day
and chases all the stars away.
That's when the farmer lifts his head
and crawls out of his cozy bed.

The morning's bright, the day is new
and on his farm there's work to do.
One cow to milk, two pigs to feed,
six ducks and hens to toss some seed.

His farm's awake with oinks and moos.
His quacking ducks no longer snooze.
His clucking chickens stretch their legs
and proudly show off newborn eggs.

But just before he starts his chores,
he hears the rumbly sound of snores.
The noise comes from his flock of sheep
out in the meadow, sound asleep.

Like fluffy lumps they lie around,
with eyes shut tight, sprawled on the ground.
Some on their backs, some on their fronts,
they toss and turn with snorts and grunts.

"Wake up," says Simpson to his sheep.
"The sun is up. So, no more sleep!
Wake up! Wake up, you snoozing herd!"
But they don't hear a single word.

"These stubborn sheep," the farmer sighs,
"won't open up their sleepy eyes.
But I know how to wake this crowd.
I'll make some noise, and make it loud."

He pounds on pots and pans with spoons,
then blows a horn and pops balloons.
He tweets a whistle made of tin
and plays a screechy violin.

He sings a peppy wake-up song,
then beats a drum and clangs a gong.
He wiggles in a squeaky chair,
but Farmer Simpson's sheep don't care.

The sheep still sleep with eyes shut tight.
The morning sun is hot and bright.
They look like blobs of fleecy custard.
Simpson's feeling sad and flustered.

Then suddenly a thought appears,
inside his head, between his ears.
"These sheep ignore the noise I make.
They're stubborn and refuse to wake.

I need some help to do the jobs
of waking fleecy custard blobs.
I'll find a trusty little pup
to wake these sheep and get them up."

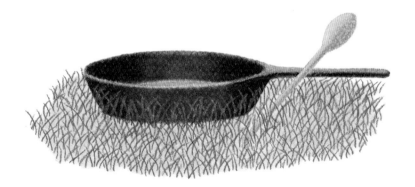

So, Farmer Simpson went and found
a puppy at the rescue pound.
He took that pup into his arms
and asked, "Do you like sheep and farms?

I have a farm that's full of sheep,
but all they want to do is sleep.
The racket of a barking pup
should wake my sheep and get them up."

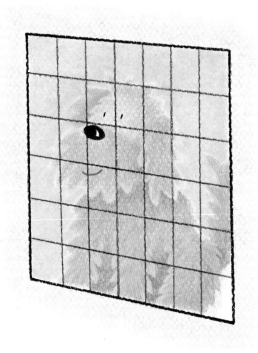

He brought that dog home to his herd
but was surprised by what occurred.
The puppy didn't bark or howl.
She didn't even whine or growl.

She tiptoed gently to the flock
as softly as her paws could walk.
She wasn't noisy, harsh, or loud,
but crept as quiet as a cloud.

With nudges from her cold, wet nose,
the sheep awoke and slowly rose,
then wandered one-by-one, away.
Some off to eat, some off to play.

They drifted up and down the hills,
among the grass and daffodils.
And with them went that gentle pup,
who from now on, would wake them up.

As Simpson watched them walk away
he said, "I've learned a better way.
That rescued puppy's gentle touch
and quiet voice have taught me much."

When friends are stubborn and won't budge,
they might need just a gentle nudge.

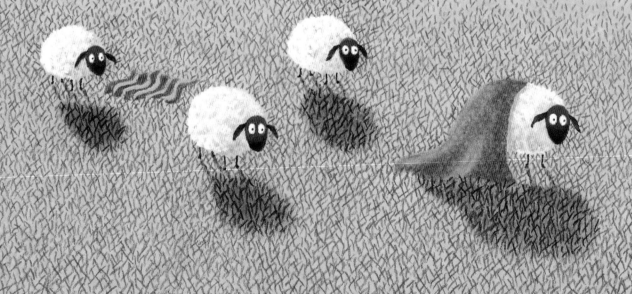